James Sutherland

NORBERT

Chapter 1

Norbert stood sheltering from the rain underneath the old sycamore tree that stood in the middle of Finbar's field. It had stopped raining two days ago but Norbert, who was never the most intelligent of horses, had failed to notice. He gazed thoughtfully at the ground beneath his hooves and saw that he had eaten every last blade of grass in that particular patch. For a moment he was baffled, but then something very unusual occurred; Norbert had a thought! *Colin the cuckoo would know what to do…* Snuggled in his nest, high up in the old sycamore tree, Colin was a wise old bird who had known Norbert ever since he was a young foal.

"Are you there, Colin?" Norbert whinnied, peering up into the leafy branches above his head.

"Of *course* I'm here!" Colin warbled from high up in his nest, a bit annoyed at being disturbed from his newspaper. "You know I'm too old to get out much these days."

"I'm sorry," said Norbert. "It's just that I've eaten all of the grass under the tree, and I'm still a bit peckish and…"

"Then move out from underneath the tree and eat some of the grass from the rest of the field, you clod-hopping clot!" interrupted Colin. "And *don't* come pestering me with any more of your silly questions!"

Norbert waddled sadly out into the May sunshine. *Why hadn't he thought of that?*

Fortunately, he was such a forgetful horse that the unpleasant episode with Colin soon vanished from his mind as he tucked into to the fresh green grass at the other end of the field.

After an hour of chomping and chewing to his heart's content, Norbert realized that he was very thirsty. He had learned over the course of his twenty-seven years in the field that whenever he was thirsty, he needed to pay a visit to the water trough, and so off he went. It was as he leaned over the stone trough to begin his drink that he saw something that made him rear up in terror. *There was another horse peering out of the water at him!* His first instinct was to trot as fast as his tired old legs would carry him back to the old sycamore tree to tell Colin what had happened, but a hazy memory in the back of his mind made him pause. *The last time he had told Colin about the strange horse in the water trough, his feathery friend had been very annoyed.* Norbert tried and tried as hard as he could to remember why…

Eventually after several minutes of intense pondering, he recalled that Colin had explained that he needn't be afraid of the horse in the water trough because it was just his own reflection.

Aha! Norbert grinned a toothy grin. *Wait until I tell Colin how clever I've been!*

First things first, though – he had better have a drink. And so, licking his big rubbery lips with anticipation, he turned back towards the trough, only to rear up in terror once again… *The strange horse was still there, peering up at him!* Already, silly old Norbert had forgotten everything he had just remembered!

A little later on, he tried again. "It's only a reflection… It's only a reflection…" he muttered as he leaned his head over the trough, closed his eyes, and began to drink the clear, cold water. When his big fat belly was too full to drink any more, he drew his head back and frowned. He waited for the ripples in the water to die down and looked again.

Was it a trick of the light? Was he seeing things? No - there was no denying the awful truth…

NORBERT'S TEETH WERE GREEN!

"Oh Colin! Colin!" he whinnied as he arrived panting and wheezing beneath the old sycamore tree "My teeth are *green*!"

"Goodness me, Norbert," came the impatient reply from above "this is hardly front page news! Your teeth have *always* been green. It's what comes of a lifetime of chewing grass and never cleaning them. Now will you kindly trot along and leave me in peace whilst I finish my crossword."

"But what will Delilah think if she sees me?" Norbert pleaded. "Her teeth are always lovely and white!"

Delilah was a pretty young pony who sometimes grazed in the adjacent field. Ever since he had set eyes on her, Norbert had been deeply in love, though he had never plucked up the courage to tell her so.

"Delilah is much younger than you, Norbert, and the little girl from the farm grooms her and cleans her teeth before the horse shows each weekend," Colin clucked. "Anyway, I thought we'd agreed that you were going to forget about that frisky filly. You know what Kipling said about the female of the species, don't you?"

"No," came the honest reply.

"He said that that they were deadlier than the male. Trust me, my friend, that girl spells trouble with a capital 'T', and you would be well advised to steer well clear of her if I were you!"

Heartbroken, Norbert waddled away, his head filled with sad thoughts. *Colin was ever so clever and was always right about everything. He was just a fat old horse. A brainless, fat old, horse. Why on Earth would a pretty pony like Delilah ever be interested in him? Yes - he would listen to Colin's advice and do his best to forget about her. Deep down, however, Norbert feared that Delilah was just about the only thing in the world he simply couldn't forget about, however hard he tried.*

"At least I still have Colin for a friend," he murmured as he plodded away to a far corner of the field.

"And *don't* go thinking you can hang around with me, either," came a grouchy voice from high up in the branches of the old sycamore tree.

Chapter 2

"Colin? Are you there?" It was the next morning and Norbert was back in his favourite spot underneath the old sycamore tree.

"Yes?" chirruped a voice from above.

"I've been thinking..."

"Really, Norbert? I must say I find that *very* hard to believe. Now, if you don't mind pushing along..."

"No, Colin," Norbert replied doggedly. "It's *true*; I *have* been thinking, all night long."

There followed a great deal of rustling as the cuckoo made a clumsy descent through the branches of the tree. Seconds later, a beaky face poked itself out from among the foliage.

"Well?" the cuckoo clucked. "And what, pray tell, have you been thinking about? The meaning of life, perhaps? Or maybe you have solved the age old question as to the origins of the universe?"

Norbert hesitated. He had a strong suspicion that Colin was not going to like what he was about to say, but he was determined to say it anyway.

"Erm no," he cringed "not *exactly*. I've been thinking that I *would* like to clean my teeth. I know what you said about Delilah, but I still think that if I had clean teeth she *might* want to talk to me and we could become friends."

"Oh, you do, do you?"

"Yes."

Hopping down from his branch, Colin landed with a *plop* on the end of Norbert's nose and fixed him with a steely glare.

"And has it occurred to you by any chance that, in order to clean your teeth, you would need a toothbrush and some toothpaste?"

"Oh?" Norbert frowned. Indeed, this had not occurred to him…

"Of course you would," the cuckoo continued "and as you do not possess either of the above, we can safely say that the matter is concluded and that this nonsense must cease."

"Eh?"

"I am *trying* to explain to you that however much you want to clean your teeth, it simply isn't possible. Now – if you don't mind, I'll be heading home to finish the crossword I was doing before I was so rudely interrupted."

And with these words, Colin hopped from his perch on the horse's nose and set off on the short-haul flight back up to his nest.

Baffled, Norbert looked around in dismay. It was a beautiful morning, the bright sunshine warming his flanks, a gentle breeze tickling his tangled mane, making the dandelions dance along the bottom of the hedgerow. And yet at that moment, he felt sadder than he had ever done before in his whole life. Absent-mindedly, he wandered over to the five-bar gate that separated his field from Delilah's. There was no sign of her today; she must be away at a horse show - a good thing as he desperately didn't want her to see him while his teeth were still green. He was about to waddle back over to the water trough for another look at them when something truly astonishing occurred;

Norbert had *another* thought! For almost an hour he stood motionless as, from tiniest grain in the back of his mind, this thought grew and grew, finally blossoming into a dazzling rainbow of hope that sent a shiver through his whole body. *At last!* For the first time *ever* in his life, Norbert had had an *idea*! But wait...this was more than just an idea... against all the odds, he had actually come up with a *plan*!

*

"Colin?"

"Yes, Norbert?"

"I'm back."

"Yes, – I gathered that. And how can I be of assistance?"

"I've been thinking again."

"Look! How many times do I have to tell you..."

"No, Colin. I really have been thinking. I *am* going to clean my teeth but I need *you* to help me."

"Norbert *please* try and understand. You don't have a toothbrush or any toothpaste.

Neither do I. Your owner, Farmer Finbar, is a mean and grumpy old so-and-so who would *never* in a million years think to give your teeth a clean. What's more, you are shut up in a field. The gate is closed and you can't possibly get out in order to obtain a toothbrush. And there I rest my case."

"But…"

"Goodbye, my friend – don't forget to write."

"But…"

"Farewell. Au revoir. Adios."

There followed what is sometimes referred to as a *pregnant* silence as Norbert pondered the situation.

"Colin?"

"Yes?"

"Can you fly?"

"Of *course* I can fly. What do you think I am? I'm a cuckoo, you know – not some species of penguin!"

"I was thinking that, if you can fly, then you could fly away and find a toothbrush and some toothpaste for me."

"That is the most *ridiculous* suggestion I have *ever* heard."

"But why?"

"Well...Well... I... I..."

Norbert peered up into the dense foliage, a glimmer of hope swelling in his heart. *If he could only persuade Colin to go along with his plan...*

"Farmer Finbar's house is just up on the hill over there. I can see that he has some of those window things open because it's such a hot day. You could easily fly in through one of them and borrow a toothbrush and some toothpaste for me."

"Oh – I could, could I?"

"Yes, Colin - you could."

For a moment, it was the cuckoo's turn to be baffled.

"Well I c… can't," he stammered. "I can't because... Because I'm feeling a little bit under the weather today and need to rest. Yes that's it – I need to rest. Awfully sorry about that, but there it is."

Norbert knew that it was now or never. *The moment had come for him to play his trump card.*

"If I had clean teeth and made friends with Delilah, I could talk to her every day and wouldn't need to disturb you again, ever."

A stunned silence from above.

"N... Not disturb me again?"

"No, Colin."

"Ever?"

"No, Colin."

"Let me get this straight, Norbert. You are saying that if I were somehow able to purloin a toothbrush and clean your teeth, allowing you to strike up a warm and loving friendship with Delilah, you would then be prepared to leave me alone? Forever?"

"Yes, Colin."

"Forever and ever Amen?"

"Yes, Colin."

"Right ho! Clear the runway – standby for take-off - I'm coming down!"

Chapter 3

Colin's descent from the sycamore tree was a harrowing spectacle which did not bode well for the mission ahead. First there came a violent rustling sound from high up in the branches. This was immediately followed by a strangled 'squawk,' as something plump and feathery emerged from the foliage in a steep downward trajectory, hurtling like a meteor towards the ground below.

"Colin?"

"Yes?" came the winded reply.

"Are you *sure* you can fly?" Norbert stood peering down anxiously at his friend who was now lying in a crumpled heap between his front hooves.

"Of *course* I can fly!" Colin gasped. "Everyone knows that the cuckoo flies south each winter to enjoy the warming African sun."

Norbert shuffled his hooves uneasily. For as long as he could remember, Colin had spent every single winter in his nest in the sycamore tree, but he was worried that pointing this out would only make his feathered friend even angrier.

"Is it nice in Africa?" he ventured tactfully.

"Well... I must confess I haven't been down there for a year or two. It *is* a bit of a trek after all, and when you get to my age, it's important not to overdo these things. Anyway, enough of this chit-chat," he clucked, eager to change the subject as quickly as possible. "I have daring deeds to perform. Now stand aside while I prepare for take-off."

"I have daring deeds to perform," said Colin. "Now stand aside while I prepare for take-off."

Again, Norbert studied his friend with concern. Though Colin *was* unquestionably a cuckoo, a species of bird capable of flying thousands of miles each year, there was something about him that did not seem *quite* right. Whereas a fit and healthy cuckoo has a long, straight tail, Colin's was a crooked affair which seemed to stick out at a peculiar angle. And whilst a healthy cuckoo has pointed, streamlined wings like a fighter jet, Colin's looked tatty and misshapen, like a World War I bi-plane that has been machine-gunned from the trenches below.

"Maybe we should think of a different plan," Norbert began, but he was too late.

Ignoring his plea, the cuckoo suddenly lurched into motion and began to taxi unsteadily along a strip of flattened grass that was to serve as a runway. Norbert could only look on in growing alarm as his friend rapidly picked up speed before launching himself skywards with a strangled *squawk!* To his amazement, the plump cuckoo somehow managed to remain in the air, feverishly flapping his wings, pitching and wheeling wildly from side to side.

"Gug, gug , gug, gug!" Colin cried as he swooped high above the horse's head.

"Pardon?" Norbert replied, squinting up into the sunshine.

"It's the sound that the common cuckoo makes when agitated," Colin explained "and believe me, I am *seriously* agitated right now. If I'm not back within the hour, please inform my next-of-kin that I perished nobly in the field of duty. I would like to request a quiet funeral ceremony with only close family present. No flowers, please."

And with these chilling words, he flew off in the direction of Finbar's farmhouse. Norbert watched as his friend headed away into the distance until he became nothing more than a speck on the horizon. A plump, odd-looking speck, but a speck nonetheless.

Unsure about how to pass the time before his friend returned, Norbert lowered his head and began to munch away at a clump of long grass. He had barely finished his first mouthful when he paused. Growing ever-louder, he could hear a noise. It was a chugging, whirring sort of a noise; the sound of a motor car engine. Raising his head, he gazed across the fields to the old lane and was dismayed to see a car heading in his direction, towing what was clearly a small, pink horsebox.

"Delilah," he gibbered despairingly *"and my teeth are still green!"*

He watched, transfixed, as the vehicle drew ever nearer, finally grinding to a halt by the gate of the adjacent field. Both car doors opened and a little girl hopped excitedly out of the passenger side, chatting happily to her father who emerged stiffly from the driver's seat sporting a smart, green wax jacket. He had the air of a man who belonged in a suburban semi-detached house, but who enjoyed indulging his daughter's hobby at weekends as this allowed him to briefly imagine himself in the role of a country Squire. They conversed for a few seconds before the man began to unfasten the sturdy metal catches that secured the door of the horse box. Norbert goggled in rapt wonder as, with the uncanny grace of a supermodel on a catwalk, Delilah trotted down the ramp towards her owner. Slimy green dribble dripped from Norbert's lower lip as he watched the little girl gently stroking Delilah's golden mane before giving her a carrot, closely followed by a sugar lump. Glancing at his watch, her father mumbled something about needing to be home in time for the football game on TV and so, having given Delilah another hug, the little girl hopped back into the car. Seconds later, there was a rumble of an engine and they were gone.

For a moment, Delilah stood and watched as the car disappeared into the distance. Norbert glanced around anxiously. He loved Delilah and *did* want to talk to her, but *not* until his teeth had been cleaned. Although she was in a different field, there was only a low hedge separating them, and he realized to his dismay that he would be clearly visible wherever he stood. There were some rather large badger holes down at the bottom of Finbar's field, near the pond, but he was fairly certain that he would not fit into any of these. Anyway, the badgers were notoriously grumpy old things and would not take kindly to a horse trying to join them their cosy set. Indeed, the only possible feature that offered any sort of cover was the sycamore tree. Though it was a very large tree with a wide trunk, Norbert was much too fat to fully conceal himself behind it, but it would at least provide *a little* camouflage. *Yes! Delilah would never spot him there: he would stand still and silently beneath its leafy branches until Colin returned with the toothbrush and toothpaste.*

"Oh Norbert! Cooey!" came a musical voice from the gate of the next field. Delilah had immediately noticed his large rotund belly protruding around each side of the tree trunk. Panic-stricken, Norbert did the only thing he could think of, which was to pretend he hadn't heard her.

"Oh Noooooorbert!" she hollered, much louder this time. "Yoo hooo!"

Unable to ignore her any longer, Norbert raised his head and turned slowly towards the sound of her voice. Even from fifty yards away, he could clearly see the sun glinting off her dazzling white teeth.

"Hello Delilah." Norbert spoke like a bad ventriloquist, moving his lips as little as possible lest she should catch a glimpse of his mouldy molars.

Delilah was puzzled, if not a little offended. Usually Norbert would trot across to talk to her as soon as she came home. *Had he gone off her? Had he fallen for another filly?*

Norbert needed to think quickly. Unfortunately, thinking quickly was not one of his strongest points.

"Why don't you come over to the gate?" Delilah whinnied happily, craning her neck as far as she could over into Norbert's field. "Then we can catch up without having to shout at the top of our voices."

Norbert began to panic.

"I've erm... I've got a bit of a sore leg today," he cringed "so I think it's best if I stay over here for the time being."

The distance between the two horses, combined with Norbert's determination not to reveal even a glimpse of his teeth rendered his feeble excuse completely unintelligible to Delilah.

"I *do* wish you wouldn't mumble so, Norbert. I'm only trying to be friendly, but if you don't want to see me, then you can suit yourself, old misery guts!" she snapped before turning and cantering off to the furthest end of her field in a huff.

Chapter 4

Meanwhile, up at Finbar's farmhouse, Colin had alighted silently on the roof of the front porch and was busy carrying out a detailed reconnaissance of the enemy terrain. At least, this was the version of events that he later gave to Norbert when recounting his daring deeds to the gullible horse. In truth, he had flown hurtling and out of control towards the house and had struck a pane of glass in the porch doorway with an almighty *thump.* Rendered completely senseless by the collision, he had then proceeded to drop like a brick onto the concrete doorstep where he reposed lifelessly for almost half-an-hour, his stumpy yellow legs sticking straight up in the air. When he came to, it took him a further fifteen minutes to remember who he was, where he was, and why he was there.

Little did Colin know that this was merely the beginning of the multiple misfortunes that fate had in store for him that day. Tragically, he had chosen to undertake his heroic mission on a Friday. Friday, alas, just happened to be the day when, after a hard week's work, Farmer Finbar liked to take a long, hot soak in the bathtub. Like many people, Finbar kept his bathtub in the bathroom, the *very same* room that housed his toothbrush and toothpaste.

"Aaaaaaaah," the farmer grunted contentedly as he lowered his bulky frame into the warm, bubbly water. A grubby individual at the best of times, Finbar had earlier that morning cleaned out both the henhouse *and* the pigsty, and for this reason he was *even* dirtier and smellier than normal. For some moments he lay in a state of bliss, wallowing like a pink walrus in the hot suds, a large flannel draped over his face, his fat belly protruding like a small island above the frothy surface of the water as he dreamed happy dreams about a string of sausages in the fridge downstairs that he had earmarked for his supper. Then came the noise…

It was a light, fluttering, flapping kind of noise, and it came from the vicinity of the open window. For a split second, Farmer

Finbar froze, still and silent, largely submerged beneath the soapy suds. Then came another flutter. And another. Very slowly, his heart beating like a drum, he peeled the flannel back from his bright red face, and what he saw almost made his piggy eyes start from their sockets.

There was a bird… A bird in his bathroom! Nay – not just any bird… It looked like a cuckoo… A fat cuckoo! Goodness me - there was a fat cuckoo in his bathroom! He continued to goggle in silent amazement. *What was it doing now? It was using its beak to remove his toothbrush from the china pot on the sink…* His mouth agape, Finbar watched as the bird proceeded to flutter back across to the window and drop his toothbrush out on to the ground below before repeating the procedure with his tube of toothpaste.

So absorbed was Colin in his task that he was completely unaware of the danger that lurked beneath the soapy suds, and it thus came as a nasty shock when, from the vicinity of the bathtub in the corner of the room there came an almighty roar.

"Very slowly, his heart beating like a drum, he peeled the flannel back from his bright red face, and what he saw almost made his piggy eyes start from their sockets…"

"GARN!" Finbar bellowed as he emerged from the bathwater like a Kraken from the deep. Soap-suds poured like a waterfall from his enormous belly, his face bright purple with rage as he clambered clumsily out onto the bathmat.

"*GAAAAARN!*" he roared again, as if to emphasize his point.

"Gug, gug , gug, gug!" Colin retorted as he flapped and fluttered around the ceiling of the bathroom, frantically trying to navigate his way towards the open window.

You may recall from earlier in the story, reader, that *gug, gug, gug, gug* is the sound that the common cuckoo makes when agitated; I think we can all agree that there are few things more likely to induce a state of agitation than being chased around a bathroom by a naked farmer who is brandishing a loofah and who is clearly intent on using it to mash you into a sort of jelly. Such was Colin's terror as he swooped and dived that he accidentally emitted a runny pellet of cuckoo droppings which struck Finbar squarely on the forehead with a loud *splat!*

"*GAAARN!*" the farmer bawled, lashing out ever more furiously with the loofah, forcing Colin to retreat into a corner of the room away from the window that offered his route to salvation. But it was in this very moment, this darkest hour when all hope seemed lost, that Lady Luck seemed to smile down on the beleaguered cuckoo. For it was now, just as Finbar was preparing to close in for the kill, that the gooey white bird droppings began to dribble down the farmer's forehead and into his eyes, temporarily blinding him. Seizing his opportunity, Colin skimmed past his deadly foe with a gleeful *gug, gug, gug, gug* and made for the open window. Rubbing his eyes and seeing his prey slipping from his grasp, Finbar made a final desperate lunge with the loofah, almost losing his balance as he did so. As he charged like a bull towards the window, he then suffered the final indignity of stepping on a bar of soap, upon which he performed what appeared to be an elaborate double pirouette on the wet, soapy tiles, before going to ground with a sickening *CRUMP*, clipping his forehead on the corner of the sink as he went down.

"Garn!" he muttered feebly as his world faded into blackness.

Chapter 5

As the sun moved steadily westwards across the sky, Norbert once again found himself standing beneath the leafy canopy of the old sycamore tree. Pondering the events of the last few hours, it seemed that he *must* be daydreaming. In the hedge that bordered the field, a host of sparrows were chitter-chattering busily among themselves in preparation for bedtime. Under normal circumstances, Norbert found these noisy little birds particularly irritating, but not today. Indeed, he did not even mind when a big hairy blue-bottle alighted on his nose and took a short stroll up his face and across his eyeball, such was his state of deepest bliss. Because today was the day when his teeth had finally been cleaned! In his long and uneventful life, he could not recall a time when he had ever felt happier.

Earlier that afternoon, things had been very different. Having watched Colin setting out on his daring mission, Norbert had been driven close to despair when, after more than an hour, there was no sign of his return. Then a speck had emerged into view on the horizon. A plump, odd-looking speck. As the speck drew nearer, Norbert could see that it was clutching something in its beak. *A toothbrush! But wait... The speck appeared to have dropped the toothbrush in a field of corn... Oh no! But what was this? The speck was diving down to retrieve it...*

When Colin finally *had* made it back to the sycamore tree and dropped the toothbrush between his friend's hooves, Norbert had studied it doubtfully. It didn't seem to have very many bristles left, and the few that remained were badly discoloured, having been used twice daily by Farmer Finbar over a period of several years, but it was still a toothbrush of sorts and would have to do.

"But what about the..." Norbert had begun, his voice bursting with anxiety.

"The toothpaste? Yes - I know!" Colin had clucked breathlessly, visibly distressed.

"I couldn't carry both, so I'm now going to have to go all the way back to Finbar's farm to get it! I did manage to drop it out of the window, so at least I will not need to risk a further foray into the Bathroom of Terror."

"Bathroom of Terror?"

"Yes. It's how I shall be referring to the bathroom at Finbar's farm from now on."

"Oh – I see."

"Now clear the runway for take-off."

Twenty minutes later, Colin had returned carrying the tube of toothpaste, looking even more haggard than before. He had, he explained, only narrowly survived an encounter with Farmer Finbar's cat, Jasper, whilst retrieving the tube from its resting place beneath the bathroom window. Norbert had noted with some sympathy that his friend appeared to have considerably fewer tail feathers than he had possessed at the outset of his mission.

If I told you that the tooth-cleaning process had been straightforward, I would be leading you astray. Indeed, it was fraught with difficulty, largely due to the fact that neither Norbert (being a horse) nor Colin (being a cuckoo) possessed anything that could accurately be described as 'hands'.

Next time you clean your teeth, try doing so without using your hands and you will gain some understanding of the sheer enormity of the task that confronted the two friends on that sunny afternoon in May.

Over a period of several hours, they tried and tested innumerable schemes and stratagems in a bid to clean Norbert's teeth, each failing to produce the desired results. There is a well-known saying that states "*If at first you don't succeed, try, try and try again.*" Norbert and Colin had never heard this saying, but nevertheless they tried, tried and tried again. And again. And again.

To describe the final method whereby they finally *did* manage to clean Norbert's teeth would require several very long and complicated chapters, so I shall merely mention that it involved the use of a plank of wood, a piece of barbed wire, nine hedge-sparrows, a rusty baked-bean tin, a length of old rope and an extremely unhappy badger.

Well reader - work it out for yourself...

Chapter 6

It was with a mixture of excitement and trepidation that Norbert approached the trough in order to study his reflection. Colin had assured him that his teeth *were* clean, but cuckoos are not always the best judges in matters of dental hygiene.

His friend had long since retired to his nest, high up in the branches of the old sycamore tree. The whole affair had undoubtedly taken its toll on the ageing bird and the loud snoring sounds from up in the dense foliage were drifting far and wide, carried across the fields on the gentle May breeze. Otherwise, apart from the occasional buzzing of a bumble bee going about his daily chores, all was quiet in Finbar's Field.

Norbert turned his gaze across to Delilah's paddock. She appeared to have forgotten about their earlier unpleasant exchange, and was now standing in a sunny spot close to the five bar gate that separated their fields.

This was it - the moment of truth! The moment upon which his entire future would depend!

Squinting at the shimmering surface of the water, Norbert leaned over the trough and drew back his pink, rubbery lips. He blinked. And blinked again... *It could not be... Or could it? Yes – the truth was undeniable...*

NORBERT'S TEETH WERE WHITE!

Some people believe that a horse's face is not capable of expressing emotions or feelings; these people are wrong. Norbert's face as he trotted across the field towards the five bar gate where Delilah awaited him was every bit as expressive as that of any human being. Indeed, it could be said that he grinned like no horse had ever grinned before. There are, of course, different types of grins. There are cheeky grins; there are friendly grins; there are crafty grins. Unfortunately for Norbert, *his* grin resembled that of a raving lunatic, his lips pulled right back over his teeth, the sheer concentration required to maintain his bizarre expression leaving him cross-eyed.

"Hi Norbert!" Delilah called brightly, noticing his waddling approach.

"Hi Norbert!" Delilah called brightly, noticing his waddling approach. "So you've decided to come and see me after all. I was just wondering if you fancied... Oh..." She stopped mid-sentence, gaping at the dazzling dentures on display before her, Norbert looking on in dismay and confusion as the smile froze on Delilah's face and then vanished.

"Oh, Norbert! How *could* you?" she squealed.

"B... B... But... I... I thought..."

"Look at your teeth! They're *white*!"

"Y...Yes...Well I just thought..."

"You thought you would show me up didn't you? By having teeth that were whiter than mine! How *dare* you! I shall *never, ever* speak to you again!"

And with these words, she turned and galloped furiously away to the farthest corner of her field.

For several minutes, Norbert stood as still as a statue before turning and waddling back to his favourite spot in the shade of the old sycamore tree.

"Are you awake, Colin?" he whinnied sadly.

"I am now, Norbert."

The cuckoo listened in rapt horror as the full details of the difficult encounter with Delilah were relayed to him.

"But things could always be worse, Colin," Norbert ended with rising optimism in his voice.

"How do you mean?" came the suspicious reply.

"Well – at least I still have one friend...YOU!"

There was a lengthy pause, followed by a *gug, gug, gug, gug* so loud that it could be heard in several adjoining counties.

This, reader, in case you have forgotten, is the sound that the common cuckoo makes when agitated.

Epilogue

Farmer Finbar awoke with a shiver. *Where was he?* It was pitch dark and he was lying on a cold, hard floor in a puddle of soapy water. His head throbbed as he tried in vain to piece together the events of the day. Rising unsteadily, he groped around the walls for the light switch, wincing in agony as the bright strip light on the bathroom ceiling illuminated the room. *What had happened? Had he been drinking a little too much home-made cider again?* He reeled a little, clutching at the sink for support. Gripping the porcelain firmly with both hands to steady himself, it occurred to him that there was something different about the sink. Something that was usually there, but which had mysteriously disappeared. *What could it be?* Then came the realisation: *his toothbrush and toothpaste were missing!* He blinked twice and splashed a little cold water on his face. Slowly but surely as his thoughts unscrambled, the high drama that had earlier unfolded in that very room came flooding back to him... *There had been a bird... A cuckoo... No... It had been a FAT cuckoo... In his bathroom, stealing his toothbrush and toothpaste. But no... That was surely impossible... Cuckoos stealing dental products? That just didn't happen... Or did it?*

"Sometimes I wonder if you're losing your marbles, Finbar," he muttered as he turned to head for the bedroom. "You must have taken that there toothbrush downstairs without meaning to. That bump on the head is making your memory play tricks on you, I reckon."

Half way to the bathroom door, he stopped. There was something stuck to the sole of his foot. In his heart of hearts, Finbar knew immediately what it was, but hardly dared to look. Still dazed, half wondering whether he was still in the middle of a bad dream, he stooped down and peeled the object from his foot.

"*GARN!*" he cried, goggling in utter disbelief. For there in the palm of his hand, soggy, grey and crooked, but unmistakable nonetheless, lay a feather. A feather that looked suspiciously like it might have once belonged to a fat cuckoo...

The End

Other titles in the

Norbert the Horse

series

Norbert's Summer Holiday

Christmas with Norbert

Norbert to the Rescue

Norbert's Spooky Night

Norbert – the Novel!

Norbert – The Collection

Other titles by James Sutherland

Ernie

Ticklesome Tales

Princess Petrina and the Witch's Curse

Frogarty the Witch

The Tale of the Miserous Mip

Roger the Frog

The Further Adventures of Roger the Frog

Jimmy Black and the Curse of Poseidon

Visit **www.jamessutherlandbooks.com**
for more information and all the latest
news!

About the Author

James Sutherland was born in Stoke-on-Trent, England, many, many, many years ago. So long ago, in fact, that he can't remember a single thing about it. The son of a musician, he moved around lots as a youngster, attending schools in the Isle of Man and Spain before returning to Stoke where he lurked until the age of 18. After going on to gain a French degree at Bangor University, North Wales, he toiled at a variety of regular office jobs before making a daring escape through a fire exit in order to concentrate on writing silly nonsense full-time. Happily married, James lives with his wife and daughter in a small but perfectly formed market town in Staffordshire. In his spare time, James enjoys playing his guitar, reading history books, and discussing the deep, philosophical mysteries of life with his goldfish, Tiffany.

Printed in Great Britain
by Amazon